MATTHEW TKACHUK

HOCKEY SUPERSTAR

BY ROY RATHBURN

Book design by Jake Nordby
Cover design by Jake Nordby

Photographs ©: Matt Krohn/AP Images, cover, 1; Bruce Bennett/Getty Images Sport/Getty Images, 4–5, 6, 26; Tim Vizer/Icon Sportswire, 8–9; Richard T. Gagnon/Getty Images Sport/Getty Images, 10; Claus Andersen/Getty Images Sport/Getty Images, 13; Rocky W. Widner/NHL/Getty Images Sport/Getty Images, 14–15; Derek Leung/Getty Images Sport/Getty Images, 17; Richard Rodriguez/Getty Images Sport/Getty Images, 18; John Woods/The Canadian Press/AP Images, 20–21; Adam Hunger/AP Images, 22–23, 30; Maddie Meyer/Getty Images Sport/Getty Images, 25; Red Line Editorial, 29

Press Box Books, an imprint of Press Room Editions, Inc.

ISBN
978-1-63494-876-0 (library bound)
978-1-63494-894-4 (paperback)
978-1-63494-928-6 (epub)
978-1-63494-912-5 (hosted ebook)

Library of Congress Control Number: 2023923040

Distributed by North Star Editions, Inc.
2297 Waters Drive
Mendota Heights, MN 55120
www.northstareditions.com

Printed in the United States of America
082024

About the Author

Roy Rathburn is a retired English teacher and former hockey player, coach, and official, from northern Minnesota.

TABLE OF CONTENTS

CHAPTER 1
Right on Time 5

CHAPTER 2
Born to Play Hockey 9

CHAPTER 3
Feeling the Heat 15

SPECIAL FEATURE
A New Career Mark 20

CHAPTER 4
Clutch Tkachuk 23

Timeline • 28
At a Glance • 30
Glossary • 31
To Learn More • 32
Index • 32

19
CCM
SHERWOOD
FLORIDA
19
BAUER

1 RIGHT ON TIME

Matthew Tkachuk was exhausted. He and his Florida Panthers teammates had been playing hockey for nearly 140 minutes. But this was Game 1 of the 2023 Eastern Conference Finals. And they still had work to do.

Less than a minute remained in the fourth overtime period. The Carolina Hurricanes tried to play the puck out of their own zone. However, a bad pass left the puck at Tkachuk's skates. Now it was time for the veteran forward to pounce.

Matthew Tkachuk's four game-winning goals during the 2023 playoffs were the most in the NHL.

FLORIDA
19
A
BAUER
SUPER TACKS

Known for his accuracy, Tkachuk picked out a corner. He fired a wrist shot over the goaltender's left shoulder. At nearly two o'clock in the morning, Florida had taken a 1–0 series lead.

The home crowd in Carolina fell silent. The only sounds came from Panthers players. They cheered as they poured off the bench. Tkachuk had other ideas. He pointed toward the exit and skated off the ice. He knew the Panthers would be playing again in just two days.

HISTORICALLY LONG

Game 1 of the 2023 Eastern Conference Finals was one of the longest games in National Hockey League (NHL) history. It had 79 minutes, 47 seconds of overtime. It was the longest game ever for both the Panthers and the Hurricanes. Only five games in NHL history had lasted longer.

Tkachuk's teammates surround him to celebrate his overtime goal against the Hurricanes.

NHL

2 BORN TO PLAY HOCKEY

Hockey impacted nearly every part of young Matthew Tkachuk's life. He was born on December 11, 1997, in Scottsdale, Arizona. That was where his dad, Keith, played for the Phoenix Coyotes. When Matthew was three, the family moved to Missouri after the St. Louis Blues traded for Keith.

Keith Tkachuk played in the NHL for 18 years. He was one of the greatest American players ever. Matthew and his brother, Brady, attended Keith's practices

Matthew Tkachuk (far left) poses with his family at Keith's (top center) final NHL game.

Matthew Tkachuk scored 52 goals in his two seasons with the US NTDP.

and games. Hockey was a way of life in the Tkachuk house.

Some of Keith's Blues teammates even lived with the family. Young players who aren't yet permanent NHL players often live with older teammates temporarily. Matthew and

Brady got to see firsthand what it took to be an NHL player.

St. Louis was a great place for Matthew to develop as a hockey player. He had a former NHL player for a coach. He also played with future NHL players such as Clayton Keller and Luke Kunin. At the age of 16, Matthew scored 82 points in 41 games.

In 2013, Matthew earned a spot among the best American players on USA Hockey's National Team Development Program (NTDP). He played two seasons for the NTDP as he grew into one of the best prospects in the country.

AMERICAN GOLD

While with the NTDP, Matthew Tkachuk got the chance to represent his country in international tournaments. At the 2015 Under-18 World Championship, Matthew led the tournament with 10 assists. He assisted on the game-tying goal in the gold-medal game against Finland. Team USA went on to win the game and the tournament.

Matthew scored 96 points in his second NTDP season while playing alongside future NHL stars such as Auston Matthews.

Matthew received an offer to play college hockey at the University of Notre Dame. But instead, he chose to play junior hockey in Canada. His team, the London Knights, was known for producing NHL stars, including Patrick Kane. Matthew played on a line with future pros Mitch Marner and Christian Dvorak.

Even on a talented team, Matthew stood out. He led the Knights to the league championship game. In overtime of that game, he sent a rocket of a shot past the goalie to win the title.

Matthew's status as an NHL prospect grew. He was ranked as one of the top skaters in North America. He followed in his father's

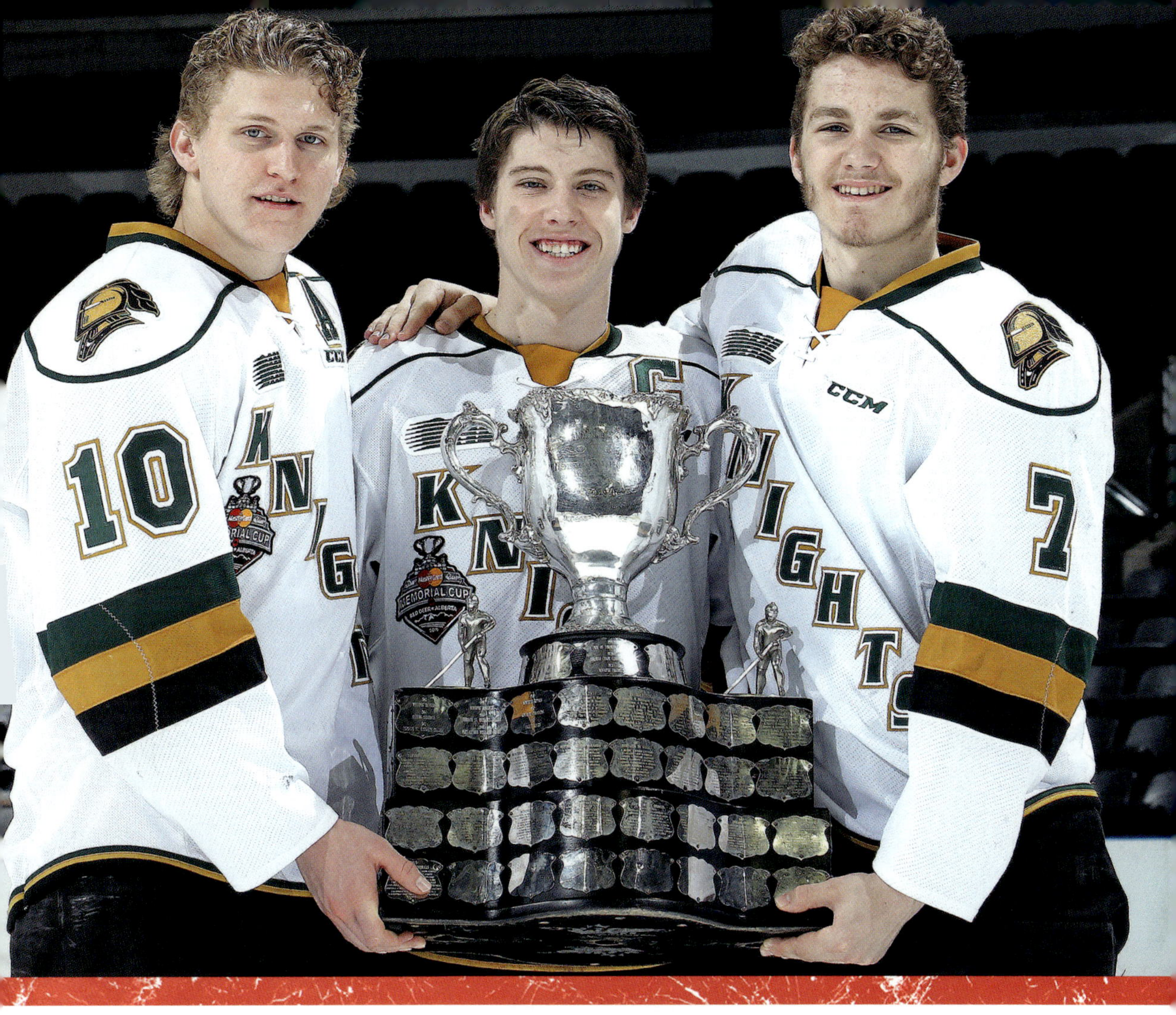

Matthew Tkachuk (right), Mitch Marner (center), and Christian Dvorak (left) hold the Memorial Cup in 2016.

footsteps as a first-round pick. The Calgary Flames chose Matthew sixth overall in the 2016 draft.

BAUER
19
BAUER
BAUER
CCM
Reebok
KAISE
PERM

3 FEELING THE HEAT

Most draft picks need time to improve before joining the NHL. But Matthew Tkachuk was different. He was ready for the big leagues right away.

It took Tkachuk just four games to score his first NHL goal. Against the Buffalo Sabres, he fired a perfectly placed wrist shot to beat the goalie. The goal tied the game, and Calgary went on to win in overtime.

Tkachuk possessed many elite skills. He had a great shot. He had great vision

Tkachuk celebrates after scoring a goal during his rookie season.

and could set up teammates to score. But what really set him apart was his size and strength. At 6-foot-2 (188 cm) and 201 pounds (91 kg), Tkachuk could play with a physical edge to his game. He wasn't afraid to go into the corner to check an opponent or dig out a puck.

Sometimes, Tkachuk was a bit too physical. In his rookie season, he was suspended two games for elbowing a player in the face. The next season, he received two more suspensions. Playing physical was a key part of Tkachuk's game. But he had to learn not to take it too far.

After his rookie season, Tkachuk started to reduce his penalty minutes. He was scoring more goals each season as well. But he could rarely make it through a season without missing games due to injuries. By 2021–22, Tkachuk

Tkachuk regularly used his big frame to check opponents into the boards.

was entering his sixth season in the league. And he still hadn't lived up to his pre-draft hype. Calgary fans were starting to worry.

Tkachuk soon put all those worries to rest. He teamed up on a line with Johnny Gaudreau and Elias Lindholm. They became one of the top-scoring lines in the NHL. Tkachuk shattered his career high in points with 104.

TELUS
11
19
A

The playoffs had been a struggle for Tkachuk. In 15 career games, he'd scored just three goals. But in 2022, he came through in big moments. In Game 7 of the opening round, Tkachuk scored the tying goal. The Flames won the game in overtime to advance to the next round.

Tkachuk followed that performance with his first playoff hat trick in Game 1 of the second round. Calgary went on to lose the series. But it was a great sign for Tkachuk's future as an offensive superstar.

BROTHERS MEET

In 2018, Matthew Tkachuk's brother, Brady, followed him into the NHL. The Ottawa Senators drafted Brady with the fourth overall pick. The brothers played each other for the first time in February 2019. Thirty members of the Tkachuk family came out to watch. Brady scored a goal, but Matthew and the Flames won the game 2–1.

Tkachuk tallied a goal and five assists against the Dallas Stars in the opening round of the 2022 playoffs.

A NEW CAREER MARK

Tkachuk scored his 42nd and final goal of 2021–22 on a breakaway. With a spray of snow, he stopped and quickly gathered a rebound to put the goal away.

CCM
19
AutoNation
19
FLORIDA
BAUER

4 CLUTCH TKACHUK

The 2022–23 season was the last year of Tkachuk's contract with the Flames. Before the season began, he started to think about whether he wanted to stay with the team long term. While Tkachuk had enjoyed his time in Calgary, he decided he was ready for a new challenge.

Five days after asking for a trade, Tkachuk became a member of the Florida Panthers. The news shocked hockey fans everywhere, especially in Calgary.

Tkachuk scored 40 goals in his first season with the Florida Panthers.

However, the Flames got multiple players in return. The Panthers only got Tkachuk. Time would tell which team won the trade.

In 2022–23, the Panthers looked like clear winners. Tkachuk set a new career high with 109 points. He also made his second All-Star team and was named Most Valuable Player (MVP) of the game. But Tkachuk shined brightest in the playoffs.

The Panthers barely made it into the playoffs. In fact, they were the lowest seed in the Eastern Conference. In the first round, Florida faced the league's best team, the Boston Bruins. Boston had set an NHL record with 63 wins. Almost no one thought Florida had a chance to beat the Bruins. The Panthers lost three of the first four games in the series. Another loss would end their season.

Tkachuk watches the puck get past two Bruins during Game 5 of their 2023 playoff series.

Tkachuk made sure that didn't happen. He scored the winner in overtime of Game 5. Afterward, he said his team would win again in Game 6. That's exactly what happened. Then the Panthers went to Boston and won Game 7 in overtime.

In the second round, Florida faced the Toronto Maple Leafs. Tkachuk didn't score

Tkachuk celebrates with his teammates after his goal sent the Panthers to the 2023 Stanley Cup Final.

in the series, but his team still came out on top. Tkachuk then played a deciding role in every game of the Eastern Conference Finals. His run began in Game 1 with a goal in the fourth overtime.

Game 2 also went into overtime. And again, Tkachuk scored the winner. This time it was just 1:51 into the first extra period. In Game 3, Tkachuk assisted on the lone goal of the game. Florida looked for the sweep. In Game 4, Tkachuk scored the series winner with just five seconds left in regulation.

Florida's magical run ended with a loss to the Vegas Golden Knights in the Stanley Cup Final. But Tkachuk's new contract meant he had seven more years with the Panthers. Fans couldn't wait to see what thrilling moments he'd create next.

ALL-STAR FRIENDS

While growing up in St. Louis, Matthew Tkachuk was friends with future Boston Celtics star Jayson Tatum. In 2023, both were named MVP of their league's All-Star Game. Tkachuk won with four goals and three assists on February 4. On February 19, Tatum set a National Basketball Association (NBA) All-Star Game record with 55 points.

TIMELINE

1. **Scottsdale, Arizona (December 11, 1997)**
   Matthew Tkachuk is born.

2. **St. Louis, Missouri (March 13, 2001)**
   The St. Louis Blues trade for Keith Tkachuk. The family moves to St. Louis, where Matthew grows up.

3. **Red Deer, Alberta (May 29, 2016)**
   In his one year of junior hockey with the London Knights, Matthew scores an overtime goal to win the league championship.

4. **Buffalo, New York (June 24, 2016)**
   The Calgary Flames choose Tkachuk sixth overall in the NHL Entry Draft.

5. **Calgary, Alberta (October 18, 2016)**
   Tkachuk scores his first NHL goal.

6. **Sunrise, Florida (July 22, 2022)**
   The Florida Panthers trade for Tkachuk and sign him to an eight-year contract.

7. **Raleigh, North Carolina (May 18, 2023)**
   Tkachuk scores the winner in the fourth overtime of Game 1 of the Eastern Conference Finals, the sixth-longest game in NHL history.

MAP

3
5
4
2
7
1
6
N

AT A GLANCE

Birth date:
December 11, 1997

Birthplace:
Scottsdale, Arizona

Position: Wing

Shoots: Left

Size: 6-foot-2 (188 cm), 201 pounds (91 kg)

NHL teams: Calgary Flames (2016–22), Florida Panthers (2022–)

Previous teams:
United States National Team Development Program (2013–15), London Knights (2015–16)

Major awards: NHL All-Star Game MVP (2023), NHL All-Star (2020, 2023)

Accurate through the 2022–23 season.

GLOSSARY

assists
Passes, rebounds, or deflections that result in goals.

contract
A written agreement that keeps a player with a team for a certain amount of time.

draft
An event that allows teams to choose new players coming into the league.

hat trick
When a player scores three or more goals in a game.

junior hockey
A level of hockey in which young players can improve their skills.

line
A set of defensemen or forwards that a player typically is paired with while on the ice.

points
Statistics that players earn by scoring goals or having assists.

rookie
A first-year player.

sweep
When a team wins all the games in a series.

veteran
A player who has spent several years in a league.

TO LEARN MORE

Books

Berglund, Bruce. *Hockey GOATs: The Greatest Athletes of All Time*. North Mankato, MN: Capstone Press, 2024.

Scifo, Dan. *Calgary Flames*. Mendota Heights, MN: Press Room Editions, 2023.

Scifo, Dan. *Florida Panthers*. Mendota Heights, MN: Press Room Editions, 2023.

More Information

To learn more about Matthew Tkachuk, go to **pressboxbooks.com/AllAccess**.

These links are routinely monitored and updated to provide the most current information available.

INDEX

Boston Bruins, 24–25
Buffalo Sabres, 15

Carolina Hurricanes, 5, 7

Dvorak, Christian, 12

Gaudreau, Johnny, 17

Kane, Patrick, 12
Keller, Clayton, 11
Kunin, Luke, 11

Lindholm, Elias, 17
London Knights, 12

Marner, Mitch, 12
Matthews, Auston, 12

Ottawa Senators, 19

Phoenix Coyotes, 9

St. Louis Blues, 9–10

Tatum, Jayson, 27
Tkachuk, Brady, 9, 11, 19
Tkachuk, Keith, 9–10
Toronto Maple Leafs, 25

Vegas Golden Knights, 27